# You
## Deserve to be
# Loved

# You Deserve to be Loved

## DR. KIMBERLY LOBERA

**ARPress**
45 Dan Road Suite 5
Canton MA 02021


Hotline:  1(888) 821-0229
Fax:        1(508) 545-7580

Ordering Information:


Quantity sales. Special discounts are available on quantity purchases by corporations,associations, and others. For details, contact the publisher at the address above.

Printed in the United States of America.

ISBN-13:   Softcover          979-8-89356-658-1
                 eBook               979-8-89356-659-8

Library of Congress Control Number: 2024903457

# CONTENTS


DEDICATION ............................................................ iii

INTRODUCTION ........................................................v

CHAPTER ONE

    HISTORY OF DATING.................................................. 1

CHAPTER TWO

    ISSUES OF ENTANGLMENT ...................................... 4

CHAPTER THREE

    LISTEN TO YOUR INTUITION.................................. 11

CHAPTER FOUR

    LEARN FROM THE PAST ...................................... 14

CHAPTER FIVE

    SO, YOU'RE SINGLE ...................................... 18

CHAPTER SIX

    PREPARE TO DATE ...................................... 22

CHAPTER SEVEN

    THE ABUSIVE CYCLE.................................... 30

CHAPTER EIGHT

    ABUSIVE RELATIONSHIPS .................................... 35

CHAPTER NINE

    TYPES OF ABUSE.................................... 39

CHAPTER TEN

    PSYCHOLOGICAL PERSPECTIVE ......................... 43

CHAPTER ELEVEN

    COMPATIBILITY ............................................... 61

REFERENCES ......................................................... 75

# DEDICATION

I would like to thank God for being a guiding force in my life.

# INTRODUCTION

This book is meant to help anyone, who is single. Regardless of why you are single, you will eventually venture back into the dating world. The problem does not lie in the fact that you are a little older and more experienced, but instead in the fact that the dating world is very different today than it was five, ten or more years ago. The electronic age has changed how people meet and interact, especially when it comes to dating.

Many websites now support the process of dating. They advertise that they have taken the work out of finding a compatible partner and that may be true, but there is something to be said for chemistry, a magnetic pull to someone, an emotional connection, or soul recognition. No website can identify these very specific elements of a relationship based upon their simplified question/answer process.

Additionally, these websites do not identify red flags that you must be cognizant of throughout the dating process. Maybe someday soon, the websites will surpass their current capabilities and be able to point out personality traits and behavioral patterns that could be an issue in a relationship. Unfortunately, the dating websites operate through the utilization of surface level information. Hence, the concept of the business intelligence model of finding a product, service, or person you desire will only be effective for supplying you with a vast array of choices.

Regardless, you must still employ your discernment to determine, if the individual meets your standards and does not have many red flags that make you want to run in the opposite direction.

The probability of finding that special someone the first time you go on a date is dubious. But in some cases, fate has an interesting way of surprising us. Just when you least expect it, that special someone can show up in your life in the most curious ways. Have you ever spoken with couples, who have been together for ten, twenty, or thirty years? They always have the most interesting stories about how they met. Those who utilize dating websites to find their ideal partner will not have those quirky, romantic, and interesting 'how we met' stories. Instead, there 'how we met' story will be a lackluster and will serve more as an advertisement for those websites than the magic of serendipitous romantic relationships that occur in spontaneous ways.

This book is written from a spiritual perspective in that we must work for continued improvement and growth in our lives. Hence, we should be very careful about whom we decide to allow into our lives. This is accomplished through careful observation and contemplation of our perspective partners. There is no greater accomplishment than to love oneself and to give and receive love from others, so choose your partner wisely.

Throughout this book there are reflective exercises meant to bring mindful awareness to the dating process. We attract, what we reflect out into the world. So, the goal is to seek harmony within, so it can materialize in your external world. You can meet and date many different individuals, but when you find someone, who is on your same level, it makes dating an exciting adventure, so enjoy the process.

# CHAPTER ONE
## HISTORY OF DATING

Throughout history, marriages were used to create dynasties, to form alliances between countries, and to obtain and hold power and wealth. Some cultures practice this tradition today, but most Americans choose their life partners. The utilization of free will brings the consequence of not choosing the most optimum mate, since we are sometimes too close to the situation to be mindful of the inconsistencies that others around us may readily see. Hence, you may not have an objective perspective, which allows you to see someone for who they really are, since you may be blinded by the love endorphins coursing through your body.

Unfortunately, there is not a course offered on how to choose a partner, what qualities to look for in a partner, or the danger signs to beware of if bad behaviors are revealed over time. This book is meant to fill that gap in knowledge by having you reflect upon your life and relationships. It is best to identify any possible problems long before any commitment is solidified. Commitment should only be secured, once there is a complete understanding of the other person. Hence, when you know their core beliefs, their actions and behaviors are appropriate and consistent over time, and there is equal give and take in the relationship. Additionally, there should be a level of comfort and understanding for the similarities and differences between the partners, long before marriage is ever discussed.

With the high number of divorces (44.6%) today, it is prudent to be very cautious before taking that leap of faith (Shawn, 2021). You must love yourself enough to protect your heart and wait for the right partner. If you rush into marriage, without fully knowing your partner, you may regret your choice. If you don't know them well before marrying them, they could reveal less than desirable behaviors, but at that point you could suffer emotionally and financially. This issue would be compounded if you had children with the individual. The point to be made here is that you must choose wisely prior to any long-term commitment being made. The advice to adhere would be to not fully commit to a relationship until you completely know and understand your partner.

## REFLECTIVE EXERCISE:  SUPPORT SYSTEM

Being blinded by love can make it difficult to see all aspects of our partner that may be evident to others around us. It is important to have a strong support system in place, who can help identify possible pitfalls in our life. Who are three trustworthy individuals that you could count on to tell you the cold hard truth, if you were to ask their opinion?

1. ________________________________________________

2. ________________________________________________

3. ________________________________________________

# CHAPTER TWO
## ISSUES OF ENTANGLMENT

All too often, people confuse lust for love and end up in bad situations with long-term consequences such as children, financial devastation, or just a general dissatisfaction in life. The confusion created by lust is that when individuals have an emotional connection toward each other it creates an energetic strand between them. This strand is strengthened when they have sex. At this point, the energetic cord is like an umbilical cord that allows for an exchange of energy between the two individuals. This cord will remain in place energetically until one or both individuals take actions to sever it (i.e., cutting the chord).

The importance of knowing about energetic cords, especially those based on sexual acts with a partner, are that they can serve as a tether to keep us tied to less than optimum people and the situations they bring into our life. Hence, sometimes we question why friends or family members stay in relationships that are clearly toxic. These people will seem to realize that there is something wrong in their relationship (i.e., manipulation, cheating, lying, abuse, etc.,), but somehow remain devoted to these people, who have questionable behavior. The reason why is that although their logic and reasoning tell them they should escape this situation, they feel bound to the individual because they are energetically tied to them. Hence, one should be extremely careful of who they engage with intimately because it can have life altering consequences that result from relationships and/or marriages that are not aligned with their highest good in life.

Being mindful of the entanglements we allow into our life is the first step toward loving ourselves. To be fully aware of others and what they bring to our life, can only enhance our ability to make informed decisions about our partner of choice and how they may impact our life. Hence, when we are led by our heart, we must be cognizant of our partner's authentic self. The problem with this task is that in psychological terms, humans display a public persona, which is not always a reflection of their true self. The warning here is that you do not become too entangled in a relationship until you have peeled back the layers of the public persona and really have a good understanding of the person's true self. Sometimes, if not always, the public persona is used as a shield to the person's darkest fears, secrets, and behaviors, which are revealed over time. Unfortunately, sometimes it takes years for the person's true nature to present itself unless you are vigilant in identifying red flags and paying attention to them.

# REFLECTIVE EXERCISE: ENTANGLEMENTS

Reflect on your previous relationship/s.

**Most previous relationship:**

Did you experience a strong connection with the individual?

_______________________________________________

How long did it take for you to get over them?

_______________________________________________

What did you have to do to get over them?

_______________________________________________

_______________________________________________

_______________________________________________

**Prior relationship:**

Did you experience a strong connection with the individual?

_______________________________________________

How long did it take for you to get over them?

_______________________________________________

What did you have to do to get over them?

_______________________________________________

_______________________________________________

_______________________________________________

**Prior relationship:**

Did you experience a strong connection with the individual?

_______________________________________________

How long did it take for you to get over them?

_______________________________________________

What did you have to do to get over them?

_______________________________________________

_______________________________________________

What was the difference between the relationships?

_______________________________________________

_______________________________________________

_______________________________________________

What coping mechanisms did you use to release yourself from these entanglements?

_________________________________________________

_________________________________________________

_________________________________________________

What lessons did you learn from each past relationship?

_________________________________________________

_________________________________________________

_________________________________________________

Did you come to the realization of an 'I'll never again' statement? If so, what were they?

I'll never again participate in…

_________________________________________________

_________________________________________________

I'll never again allow…

_________________________________________________

_________________________________________________

I'll never again date someone who…

_______________________________

_______________________________

**Positive Dating Statement**

From this day forward, I will only entertain individuals,

Who treat me with respect by…

_______________________________

_______________________________

Who are capable of…

_______________________________

_______________________________

Who (you fill in the blank)…

_______________________________

_______________________________

_______________________________

Who (you fill in the blank)…

______________________________________________

______________________________________________

______________________________________________

# CHAPTER THREE
## LISTEN TO YOUR INTUITION

Be cognizant of the individuals you entertain because they can either have a positive or negative impact on your life, so choose wisely. One area of concern would be a red flag, which in a relationship is something that you want to identify as soon as possible and consider how that element will impact you and the relationship over time. It is up to you to determine, which red flags will be deal breakers and which ones you are willing to endure. Before you decide to venture into your next relationship, take time to reflect on what you did not care for in your previous relationships. The factors that you identify will be your personalized list of red flags. Red flags can be categorized into groups such as issues that conflict with trust, respect, loyalty, broken boundaries, and balance in the relationship.

Usually, your intuition (i.e., gut feelings) will make you aware of situations that seem off. These gut feelings are usually your soul's identification of red flags. Red flags could come in the form of a comment or action that your partner says or does that makes you uncomfortable or makes a question pop up in your mind. Red flags can also be overindulgence in alcohol, drug use, jealousy, control issues, aggressiveness, deceitful behavior, lying, cheating, stealing, etc. Do not ignore the red flags because they are a way of opening your eyes to your partner's true authentic self. I'm not suggesting to question everything they say or do, only those things that your intuition brings to your awareness through gut feelings or epiphanies. If you are in a deep state of love with your partner, you may miss the warning signs that your intuition sends you. So, remember to keep yourself in a state of awareness, so your intuition can warn you of possible danger signs in your relationship. At the same time, do not engage in analysis paralysis (repetitive thoughts) in your mind, instead focus on your intuition and what it tells you.

If you are not in tune with your intuition, you could enhance it through short meditations. This does not require any skill whatsoever. Simply locate a place where you can be for about ten to fifteen minutes without interruption. Turn your phone off and remove all distractions from the space. Sit in a comfortable position with your back erect and close your eyes. Then, breathe in through your nose and out through your mouth; three times. After that, breathe normal. Simply focus on nothingness. Thoughts will race through your mind. Do not worry, simply let them flow in and out of your mind. Once they stop, then you can ask yourself questions about your partner. These could be anything that has made you feel uncomfortable while you were with your partner. Simply ask whatever you want to know and then sit quietly until you receive an answer. The answer may come in the form of a feeling, a knowing, or verbal confirmation depending upon how your intuition communicates with you.

## REFLECTIVE EXERCISE: RED FLAGS

What are the red flags that you have experienced in past relationships?

_______________________________________________

_______________________________________________

_______________________________________________

_______________________________________________

What red flags are deal breakers for you?

_______________________________________________

_______________________________________________

_______________________________________________

_______________________________________________

# CHAPTER FOUR
## LEARN FROM THE PAST

People, situations, and experiences are brought into our lives for a season or a reason. They give us the opportunity to experience different or difficult lessons that help our soul grow over time. Many people, who are spiritual believe that we are spiritual beings, who are incarnated into physical bodies, so we can learn lessons through the relationships and experiences we encounter throughout our lives. Within these lessons one of two things will occur. Either the individual will learn the lesson the first time their life experience presents it to them, and they freed to move on to learn different lessons. Or they don't learn the lesson and are caught in a loop where they will continue to repeat the same cycle (i.e., problem) again and again, until their lesson is learned. Sometimes, the same problem is played out in different relationships. Usually, individuals start to see a pattern in their life and start to question and reflect upon their relationships and the similarities between the issues among those relationships. Some of life's lessons are referred to as karmic because they are difficult to work through and difficult to move past. Eventually, most individuals finally figure out what lesson needed to be learned and they move on with their life with the wisdom learned from that experience. As a result, their soul has grown from the experience. So, be thankful for the difficulties in your life that you have been able to surpass because that means you have learned that life lesson.

Relationships are quite complex, so there is no special formula for choosing the perfect partner. Rather, it is important that you understand some of the complexities of yourself and your possible future partner. By having a good understanding of what you want or better yet you don't want in a relationship; understanding what a good relationship is; and understanding the warning signs and possible issues of specific situations, you may be able to make more informed decisions for the life-changing matter of being in a committed relationship or getting married.

Since past behavior is usually a good predictor of future behavior, it is prudent to speak with or see how your perspective partner interacts with those people closest to them. Sometimes family and friends will let information slip out that the person would not have shared. Usually, just embarrassing stories, but on occasion someone will spill the dirt either consciously or subconsciously. Either way, you obtain some information that you would not have been privy to otherwise. A word of caution here though. Sometimes, people have frenemies. For example, there family, friend, or frenemy may share that the individual has had many relationships and has cheated in most of them. This would be a huge red flag that you should take into consideration before going any further in this relationship. Every person who is currently single has obviously had some difficulty in the relationship department; otherwise, they would not be single. So don't be judgmental, just be cautious of the red flags as they present themselves to you. Then, determine whether you can live with the red flags without experiencing some sort of negative emotional reaction. Discuss your concerns with your partner and make a final call based upon the collaboration and cooperation of your partner in addressing the issues identified as being red flags.

It's not only important to understand our partner's relationship history, but to understand our own. As children, we see relationships modeled for us mainly by our parents, grandparents, or caregivers. The point to be made here is that those relationships help to define what we view as normal relationship behavior. So, if you grow up in a household where the caretaker relationship is abusive in nature; there is a strong probability that you may behave in an abusive manner in your relationships. Likewise, a home environment that models negative behaviors such as constant conflict, outbursts of jealousy, and disrespectful dialogue between caregivers sets a very negative example to be followed. As a result, we may end up in a horrible relationship because we have not set our standards high enough, we do not believe we are worthy of anything better, or we have only seen dysfunctional relationships modeled for us throughout our childhood. On the other hand, if we are cognizant that our relationship is not optimum and we escape prior to any permanent repercussions, then we have done well for ourselves. Every person has free will to choose how to behave. The behavior modeled during the childhood stage of life will more than likely be the dominant behavior displayed in relationships. Until the individual decides they want to learn a more positive perspective and incorporates behavioral adaptations that are more aligned with healthy relationship behaviors.

## REFLECTIVE EXERCISE:  BEHAVIORAL MODELING

What were the five most impactful behaviors you had modeled for you during your childhood?

_______________________________________________

_______________________________________________

_______________________________________________

_______________________________________________

From those behaviors, which ones do you use in your relationships?

_______________________________________________

_______________________________________________

_______________________________________________

If you could change your behaviors, which ones would you change and why?

_______________________________________________

_______________________________________________

_______________________________________________

# CHAPTER FIVE
## SO, YOU'RE SINGLE

Regardless of how you decide to reenter the dating world, it can be scary after you have been in a long-term relationship. All the things you learned not to care about while you had a partner are now at the forefront of what you need to consider. The comfortable life you may have had while married or in a long-term relationship is no longer your reality. Your reality now consists of having to do everything for yourself. It is not easy to readjust to being solely responsible for everything, but you can do it. It is accomplished one day at a time.

If you're newly single and you go out into public, it can be a bit frustrating to see everyone paired up, but do not let that get you down. It is important to take time to process your emotions and grieve the loss of your relationship. The grieving process is very personal in nature and will be dependent upon how and why the relationship ended and, who was more emotional invested. The individual, who carried more emotional ties in the relationship, will take longer to heal from this wound. It is admirable, mature, and healthy for someone to take the time to process their emotions, reflect upon what they could do better in their next relationship, and heal fully prior to jumping into another relationship. This helps the person to avoid repeating the same lesson again.

I have seen many people, who leave one relationship only to immediately jump into another. This can be disastrous because they are taking the underlying problems of their previous relationship/s with them into the new relationship. Not to mention, they have a major issue that they are not facing and that is an insecurity of being alone. Individuals should not jump from one relationship to another to fill the void of a missing partner. Everyone should be whole on their own or at the very least able to stand on their own without reliance on another person to find their happiness. Happiness comes from within the individual, not from their partner. When people search for their 'other half' it should not be based on the premise that the other person will make them whole, simply the other person will complement their life.

Another problem with relationship hopping is that the person is in a vulnerable state and may be emotionally blinded to who their person really is. Hence, the ability to see through the public persona may be at a disadvantage and be clouded due to emotionality. What I mean by this is, when you first start dating someone, they show you their public persona, which may or may not be a true representation of who they really are. Hence, you may not detect all the cues telling you that the great, wonderful, new person who seems to do everything right is rude, inconsiderate, and abusive. (You can fill in the blanks with the adjectives that apply to anyone you have ever dated, who turned out to be a monster in waiting.) The warning here is to be careful and not rush into any relationship too soon. Take it slow and make sure you know what kind of person you want, the qualities that you want them to possess, and how you want them to treat you. If you don't know what you want, how will you know when you've found it?

Conversely, it is sometimes faster and easier to identify what we don't like. The creation of a list that would exclude someone from your dating pool would be much easier to create and follow than an inclusionary list. Let me explain, you go to a restaurant, review the menu, and choose what you want to eat from the forty plus items available, but you know from everything that's listed the only things you needed to exclude from your ordered item is onions and peppers. This same concept can be applied to dating. The exclusions could be the person is emotional distant, immature, and rude. That is a much easier way to determine, if you want to continue to pursue a relationship with this person. On the other hand, if you utilized a list of things you want in a partner, you might never find someone, who fits your desired description.

## REFLECTIVE EXERCISE:  TO AVOID

Think back on your previous relationships. What were five things that you can identify that you do not care to see in your next relationship?

1.

__________

__________

2.

__________

__________

3.

__________

__________

4.

__________

__________

5.

__________

__________

# CHAPTER SIX
## PREPARE TO DATE

Before you venture out on that first date, you must prepare. Reentering the dating world requires that you take a personal inventory of what you've experienced in the past, identify what you do not want in your next partner, and clarify what you want to experience in your future relationship. If you don't know what you want, how can you ever get it? First, you must make an inventory of the people you have dated in the past. You could even write down the pros and cons of each person and relationship. This serves a few purposes. The first is to identify what type of person you are attracted to, are their similarities in personality, behaviors, attitudes, social status, etc. What were the commonalities of these individuals? Do you see a pattern? What did you dislike about each of them? The identification of patterns of behavior and qualities that you do not care for, will hopefully allow you to identify and avoid the pitfall of repeatedly choosing the wrong type of person for you. To stop the insane cycle of repetitive mistakes, take stock in your past and learn from it. If you keep finding the same type of person and it does not work out, get out of your comfort zone, and try a new approach such as a different way of dating, a new hobby, or try learning a new skill. Find something to be passionate about, besides being passionate. The point to be made here is that you need to expand your consciousness with experiences, so new and different types of people will be in your vicinity.

You know that you have some work to do to figure out exactly what you want in your new partner. To begin with, you need to consider differences between you and your partner because they can cause problems to erupt not necessarily in the beginning of the relationship, but later once you have invested time and energy. The reason for this is the public persona that I have already discussed. The public persona is what we let everyone see, which is usually not our true authentic self. The true self is revealed once we have established a relationship with someone. The problem is that sometimes we reveal our true selves, but our partner does not. This can be risky because we disclose too much information, and the other person withholds information. This creates an imbalance since reciprocity is absent. For example, you begin seeing a man and you share with him that you have children. Although he does not like the idea of having children or raising someone else's children, he pursues a relationship with you. In this situation, the man is wasting your time, since your children are a fundamental part of your life (or they should be). Hence, a relationship with this man would be pointless. This is an example of the public persona (i.e., the man pretending to accept you and your child) being very different from his true self.

Before you begin dating, you must determine what it is you want to gain out of a relationship. Hence, you must try to determine your level of commitment, the type of partner you want to date, the type of relationship that you want to have, and how much time and effort you're going to invest in this relationship. You need to determine what is important to you. What are your values and beliefs, and how they will impact your relationship? It sometimes helps to think back on your previous relationships and determine what problems were present and what instigated the problems. If you had relationships that have ended over differences of beliefs, you should identify what those beliefs were that you or they held so strongly because you want to make sure that your next partner has congruent beliefs and values. Or determine where you are willing to compromise. Many times, people date, fall in love, and then later find out that they have very different beliefs and values from their partner. Beliefs and values are foundational to how we view the world. If you have different values from your partner, your relationship can be difficult depending upon the disparity between the beliefs. This is a personal matter that would require a thoughtful conversation and either a compromise or an agreement to disagree respectfully.

Take a physical inventory of the values and beliefs that you hold and rate them according to their importance. Sometimes, it's a matter of knowing ourselves better in the process of trying to find a partner. I'm not suggesting that you go to find your perfect partner, who is exactly like you because that would make for a dull relationship. I am suggesting that you balance your beliefs and values with your partner's beliefs and values, so you agree on fundamental issues as opposed to being in opposition to each other. Through this process of self-awareness, you will hopefully be able to identify areas that can be improved in future relationships. To move forward in your life, you must not repeat the negative past and instead move forward with a positive outlook on life by knowing what you want and going after it.

Likewise, it is important to identify your pattern of behavior in choosing a mate and what drew you to them. Once you feel you have exhausted your reflective abilities by completing this task, you will need to review the list to determine whether your previous relationships have common threads. These common threads will help you identify the major attributes and characteristics of your type of partner. It will also help you to identify the type of partner that you want to avoid dating.

Next, by identifying the pros of your previous relationships, you can identify the qualities that you look for in your perfect mate. By knowing this information, you are going to save yourself a great deal of time in trying to sort through what you want in a partner. I'm not suggesting that you make a list and check it twice like Santa Claus and expect to find Mr. or Ms. Perfect but being aware of your preferences will help you in your search for your perfect mate. This is very insightful information that will serve you well for future relationships. This exercise will help you in determining all the qualities you look for in a partner. When referring to qualities, I am not referring to their physical looks. I am referring to qualities such as their personality, character, beliefs, values, and actions. Hence, if you meet a partner and he or she has five good qualities from your list and only one negative (depending upon what it is), you may have a viable candidate for a relationship. Only you will be able to answer the question, is this the right partner for me?

# REFLECTIVE EXERCISE:  VALUES AND BELIEFS

It is good to understand the compatibility factors in a relationship. Consider your values in determining compatibility with your partner. On a scale of 1 to 10, one being the least important and 10 being the most important, indicate how important these values and beliefs are to you:

| VALUES & BELIEFS | LEAST VALUE | | | AVERAGE VALUE | | | | | MOST VALUE |
|---|---|---|---|---|---|---|---|---|---|
| RELIGOISUS BELIEF | 1 | 2 | 3 | 4 | 5 | 6 | 7 | 8 | 9 | 10 |
| HAVING A FAMILY | 1 | 2 | 3 | 4 | 5 | 6 | 7 | 8 | 9 | 10 |
| HAVING A CAREER | 1 | 2 | 3 | 4 | 5 | 6 | 7 | 8 | 9 | 10 |
| SOCIAL SITUATIONS WITH PARTNER | 1 | 2 | 3 | 4 | 5 | 6 | 7 | 8 | 9 | 10 |
| FREEDOM IN RELATIONSHIP | 1 | 2 | 3 | 4 | 5 | 6 | 7 | 8 | 9 | 10 |
| TIME FOR SELF | 1 | 2 | 3 | 4 | 5 | 6 | 7 | 8 | 9 | 10 |
| TRUST IN RELATIONSHIP | 1 | 2 | 3 | 4 | 5 | 6 | 7 | 8 | 9 | 10 |
| RESPECT IN RELATIONSHIP | 1 | 2 | 3 | 4 | 5 | 6 | 7 | 8 | 9 | 10 |
| PARENTING STYLE | 1 | 2 | 3 | 4 | 5 | 6 | 7 | 8 | 9 | 10 |
| POLITICAL BELIEFS | 1 | 2 | 3 | 4 | 5 | 6 | 7 | 8 | 9 | 10 |

# REFLECTIVE EXERCISE: TRAITS

Consider your traits and the traits of previous partners. In addition to determining what your values and beliefs are and how highly you hold them, it is important to understand yourself and the type of person that you are. Circle the appropriate number to indicate the level of degree that you identify with this trait. On a scale of 1 to 10, 1 being the least like you and 10 being the most like you. Then, complete this exercise for your previous partner or have your current partner complete it.

| TRAIT | LEAST LIKE ME | | | SOMEWHAT LIKE ME | | | | | MOST LIKE ME |
|---|---|---|---|---|---|---|---|---|---|
| EXTROVERT | 1 | 2 | 3 | 4 | 5 | 6 | 7 | 8 | 9 | 10 |
| INTROVERT | 1 | 2 | 3 | 4 | 5 | 6 | 7 | 8 | 9 | 10 |
| RIGID | 1 | 2 | 3 | 4 | 5 | 6 | 7 | 8 | 9 | 10 |
| FREE SPIRIT | 1 | 2 | 3 | 4 | 5 | 6 | 7 | 8 | 9 | 10 |
| GOAL ORIENTED | 1 | 2 | 3 | 4 | 5 | 6 | 7 | 8 | 9 | 10 |
| FREE WILLING | 1 | 2 | 3 | 4 | 5 | 6 | 7 | 8 | 9 | 10 |
| FUN LOVING | 1 | 2 | 3 | 4 | 5 | 6 | 7 | 8 | 9 | 10 |
| RESERVED | 1 | 2 | 3 | 4 | 5 | 6 | 7 | 8 | 9 | 10 |
| SPONTANEOUS | 1 | 2 | 3 | 4 | 5 | 6 | 7 | 8 | 9 | 10 |
| PLANNER | 1 | 2 | 3 | 4 | 5 | 6 | 7 | 8 | 9 | 10 |

After completing this exercise, you will see where you fall in respect to your attributes. You must understand yourself before you can understand anyone else. Do you have more similarities or differences? Could the differences help you two to complement each other or do you think these attributes will cause issues within your relationship?

# REFLECTIVE EXERCISE:  RELATIONSHIP PROS & CONS

To begin the process of determining what you need in your next relationship, reflect on your past relationships. List the Pros and Cons of each relationship you have had, beginning with the most recent. As you go through this process, there is a high probability that the "Cons" side of the list will be filled with many comments, and the "Pros" side will more than likely be a short list. It is important that you identify both the pros and cons of your previous relationships, since this process will give insight into the type of people you are drawn to and what the major issues were that created dissonance in your relationships.

| PROS | CONS |
| --- | --- |
|  |  |
|  |  |
|  |  |
|  |  |
|  |  |
|  |  |
|  |  |
|  |  |
|  |  |
|  |  |
|  |  |
|  |  |
|  |  |
|  |  |
|  |  |
|  |  |
|  |  |

# CHAPTER SEVEN
## THE ABUSIVE CYCLE

If a person is reared in an environment that is abusive in nature, it will impact all of their future relationships. In an abusive relationship, there will be a cycle of abuse that will occur. It will involve the abuser, who will lose control and act out verbally (psychological abuse) and/or physically (domestic violence, sexual abuse, etc.) toward others. Then, there will be a period of reconciliation in which their behavior returns to normal state, but they may offer no apology to the victims and/or witness for their unacceptable behavior. This can be quite confusing to the victims and witnesses because they know that the abuser's behavior was abnormal. Although the abuser acts as if nothing was wrong with what they did. The abuser's other possible reaction could be explained as the redemption phase. In this phase, the abuser will return to a normal state of being and then will beg for forgiveness from the victims; offer gifts to win back the favor of the victims; apologize profusely and promise it will 'never' happen again. In the most deviant situations, some abusers will blame the victim by projecting the abuse back on them. For example, 'why did you make me, hit you?' Regardless, of how the abuse is inflicted, the abuser will justify their behavior as right, which will negatively impact the victims' psychological well-being. As the cycle of abuse continues over time, the victims become conditioned to the situation and, as a result, the victims learn to 'walk on eggshells' around the abuser or the victims will withdraw from interactions with the abuser because they never know what will set the abuser off and send them into a rage. This coping mechanism for the victims helps to reinforce the abuser's behavior because it allows them to maintain control of everyone in their environment.

After living in an abusive environment, victims live in a constant state of distress because there is such uncertainty in their home environment. Hence, the 'fight or flight' response is triggered. Likewise, victims begin to believe the abusive negative comments that are directed at them. They may internal the abuse and begin to feel as if they are to blame for the abuser's behavior towards them. As a result of these factors, they live in a state of distress and their self-esteem is diminished with each additional abusive occurrence. This process can help them lose hope for a happier existence, make them lack confidence in themselves, and promote feelings of unworthiness.

This pattern of abuse can continue into adulthood where the grown children still fear the abuser. Although the abuser does not hold the same level of control over their life. It is like the victim regresses back into the role of the child in the presence of the abuser. In these cases, the adult victim simply justifies the abuser's behavior and continue their lives as normal although they live with a state of fear for the abusive individual. Conversely, some victims take a different perspective on the abusive relationship and actively work to change their behavior toward the abusive parent. Instead of allowing the abusive parent to continue their method of abuse and control, the individual does not reinforce the abuse. Rather, when the abuser acts out, the grown victim calls them on their unacceptable behavior, does not walk on eggshells, and does not allow the abuser to maintain control in the situation. Hence, not reinforcing unacceptable behavior to extinguish the undesirable behavior and take control back from their abuser.

Unfortunately, after years of this maladaptive relationship behavior being modeled for them, victims can view abusive partnerships as normal unless they are exposed to alternative relationship models, which are normal in nature and lack abuse. Or, unless they have taken active steps to heal from the psychological wounds created by the abuse endured in childhood. If you were a victim of abuse during your childhood, you may suffer from a new diagnosis called Complex Post Traumatic Stress Disorder (CPTSD). "CPTSD is highly prevalent in treatment seeking populations who have been… traumatised [on multiple occasion throughout their] childhood and adulthood" (Karatzias, 2017, p. 187). CPTSD is a disorder that is similar in nature to Post Traumatic Stress Disorder (PTSD), which is characterized by reliving the traumatic experience, avoidant behavior, and a current sense of a threat in one's vicinity along with a Disturbance in Self-Organization (DSO) functional impairment, which includes "(1) affective dysregulation, (2) negative self-concept, and (3) disturbances in relationships" (Cloitre, n.d., p. 1). If you feel you may suffer from this disorder, please seek the assistance of a medically licensed professional, so they may assist you.

## REFLECTIVE EXERCISE:  JUDGING THE SELF

What are things you tell yourself that you know are not true?

________________________________________________

________________________________________________

________________________________________________

________________________________________________

Where did these ideas come from?

________________________________________________

________________________________________________

________________________________________________

________________________________________________

________________________________________________

________________________________________________

Are they true or did you simply begin to believe what someone else told you?

________________________________________________

________________________________________________

________________________________________________

________________________________________________

________________________________________________

Could you release them by transmuting them into something positive? Most things in life can be seen from a positive or a negative viewpoint depending upon the perspective. Try to change your perception of yourself to a positive perspective. Rephrase the untrue statements below in a positive manner.

__________________________________________________

__________________________________________________

__________________________________________________

__________________________________________________

__________________________________________________

__________________________________________________

# CHAPTER EIGHT
## ABUSIVE RELATIONSHIPS

There are several reasons why someone will stay in an abusive relationship. First and foremost, they may not understand that they are in an abusive relationship. This goes back to their childhood and the behavior they saw modeled for them by their caregivers (i.e., mother, father, grandparents, etc.). Hence, abusive behavior may be the norm for them, so an unhealthy relationship from their perspective is normal.

Fear may also be a deciding factor that keeps a person in an abusive relationship. The fear can be brought about through the mental, physical, or emotional scars left from past abuse. Additionally, the fear to leave may be due to threats made by the abuser such as "if I can't have you, nobody will." There have been many relationships that have ended in the disfigurement or even the death of the victim from abusers, who have lived by this mantra. Unfortunately, living with an abuser is like being a prisoner of war. You have just as much chance of being hurt from staying as you do from leaving.

An additional factor of fear that may be present is the fear of secrets being revealed. Secrets can entail past and present behaviors that might be embarrassing, if disclosed. Likewise, fear of sexual preferences or orientation being disclosed to family and friends may serve to keep a person in an abusive relationship.

The abused person may also stay in an abusive relationship if they have low self-esteem. They will feel that they cannot get anyone better or they don't believe they deserve to be treated better. Staying in an abusive relationship is a form of self-inflicted pain if the relationship is continued. Low self-esteem is not a matter that is easily solved. It can take years of reassurance and confidence building to overcome low self-esteem. A person, who has low self-esteem and is in an abusive relationship, will compound their issue of low esteem because the abusive relationship reinforces the negative feelings, they already have about themselves. After continually being told hateful and hurtful things by an abuser, the victim will begin to internalize the negative statements made and will accept them as the truth. They will not question why a person, who supposedly loves them, would say such things to them. As a result of the acceptance, these negative statements reinforce a negative self-image of the victims.

The military does something similar with new recruits in bootcamp. Not the abuse aspect, but the process of breaking an individual down. They break down recruits emotionally and physically by taking all freedoms and controlling every aspect of their lives. Then, they start building them up by teaching them lessons that will help them survive in the field. In the case of the abused person with low self-esteem, they only get broken down. Once the victim has conscious awareness that a problem exists can they take action to remove themselves from an abusive situation. When they leave the abusive relationship, they are then able to begin the healing process and start building their self-esteem.

Another aspect, which can cause fear of leaving an abusive relationship, can come from social pressures. The first type of social pressure comes from cultural beliefs. Cultural beliefs can encompass a wide range of aspects in a person's life. In many cultures, gender roles are determined and deeply ingrained as a means of norming behavior (i.e., traditional roles). Next, religion can apply an extra layer of concern for what the appropriate behavior is or is not. For example, if divorce is even an option. Finally, an abused person may fear leaving their abuser for fear of what the abuser will do to their children, family, or friends, if they leave.

Another possible reason why someone would stay in an abusive relationship would be due to economics. If the abuser does not allow the abused to get an education or get a job, then they will have a difficult time leaving and standing on their own if they do leave the situation. Hence, if the victim's economics are controlled by the abuser, they are dependent upon the abuser and will have a difficult time gaining any independence; thus, leaving becomes more difficult. The good news is that there are many resources available today that allow abuse victims to leave abusive relationships and gain their independence.

Finally, and probably the most important reason why someone will stay in an abusive relationship is that they love the person. As it has been said many times, "Love is blind."

Sometimes when an individual falls in love, they fail to see the true person they are dealing with. Hence, they are blinded to the abuse thanks to the emotional roller coaster that occurs when they fall in love. Unfortunately, it is not until much later in the relationship that the individual realizes they are in a bad situation.

Although, their friends and family may have warned them about the abusive partner not being good for them. In some cases, the victim will justify the abuser's behavior to family and friends. Once the victim has vouched for the abuser as being a 'good person' to their family and friends, it backs the victim into a corner when they eventually realize they are in an abusive relationship. Whether it is pure embarrassment, pride, or ego, sometimes victims stay in abusive relationships far too long.

# REFLECTIVE EXERCISE: SELF-INVENTORY

What are three things you would like to improve about yourself? What steps could you take to make the changes you want in your life?

1.

_______________________________________________

_______________________________________________

_______________________________________________

_______________________________________________

2.

_______________________________________________

_______________________________________________

_______________________________________________

_______________________________________________

3.

_______________________________________________

_______________________________________________

_______________________________________________

_______________________________________________

# CHAPTER NINE
## TYPES OF ABUSE

According to the Healing Abused Women organization, one-third of all American women will experience some sort of domestic abuse. Similarly, the Child Welfare Information Gateway (2003) noted several tactics utilized by abusive perpetrators, and they can include any or all the following tactics: physical, sexual, verbal, emotional, or psychological. Likewise, according to the Child Welfare Information Gateway (2003), the root causes of domestic violence are learned behaviors. For example, exposure to or personal experience with domestic violence. There are several types of abuse that occur, but regardless of which type of abuse a person is exposed to, they are all detrimental to the sense of self and personal safety. We should feel free and secure within our relationship, so we do not have to experience such things as abuse. The most common types of abuse are listed below.

### Economic Abuse

Economic abuse is the prevention of economic advancement of an intimate partner. "Financial abuse is the utilization of money or access to accounts to exert power and or control over partner" (Respect Web site, n.d., 1). This is done through the restriction of the partner from being allowed to be gainfully employed (with monitoring activities such as frequent calls or visits to the workplace and blocking attendance to school) or from being self-sufficient. Another method of economic abuse is to withhold resources; this is usually accomplished by giving the victim an allowance and then making them accountable for every cent. Likewise, the victim is kept from being financially independent by not having access to transportation, childcare or not being allowed to leave the house, which would prevent them from working.

## Emotional Abuse

Emotional abuse involves the psychological, nonphysical, verbal, or nonverbal threatening of another person. In an intimate relationship, emotional abuse can involve any or all the following behaviors directed at the victim: yelling, belittling, berating, swearing, frightening, ordering, demeaning, blaming, and humiliating. Likewise, withholding resources or affection, refusing to help the partner, restricting the partner's access to attend school and work, ability to socialize, leave home, seek medical care, or endangering the health or well-being of the partner or the partner's loved ones.

## Social Isolation

The abuser utilizes social isolation of the victim as a means of control. The abuser isolates the victim by poisoning the relationships between friends and family of the victim. Hence, the abuser eliminates the victim's social network and support system. Usually, the isolation occurs because of the abuser's jealousy, suspiciousness, and threatening behaviors. Through a series of arguments, the victim gives up socializing to appease the abuser, and in that process, the abuser gains ultimate control over the victim.

## Physical Abuse

Physical abuse is physical aggression toward another person, which threatens the person's physical safety, health, and well-being. It is the repetitive infliction of physical pain and suffering on the victim, which can result in injury or even death. Likewise, physical abuse causes deep, permanent emotional wounds, along with the physical scars left from the abuse. Physical abuse usually escalates and becomes more frequent over time. Physical abuse could include any of the following behaviors: kicking, punching, burning, strangling, threatening with a weapon, or controlling birth control choices.

## Sexual Abuse

Sexual abuse is the act of taking the choice away from the victim regarding their sexual activity. This type of abuse includes ultimatums being used to coerce the victim to engage in unwanted (i.e., rape) or dangerous sexual activity (i.e., bestiality, unprotected sex, pornography, or prostitution). This also includes the use of drugs or alcohol to manipulate the victim into sex that they would not normally engage in if they were not under the influence.

## Stalking

Stalking is the repetitious and unsolicited attention from an obsessed individual whom the victim may or may not have had a romantic relationship with in the past. Stalking is harassment, which threatens the victim's safety and peace of mind. This type of abuse is usually displayed through the following types of behaviors: verbal threats, spying, giving inappropriate gifts, destruction of property, or stealing from the victim.

## Digital Abuse

Technology has become a new medium for abuse. Digital abuse is the use of technology to ruin reputations and to taunt the victim electronically. Through social networking or texting, the victim is hassled and/or frightened (Respect Web site, n.d.).

## Myths Pertaining to Domestic Violence

According to the Child Welfare Information Gateway (2003), there are several myths pertaining to domestic violence such as "[o]nly poor, uneducated women are victims of domestic violence." The truth is that domestic violence occurs in all social and economic classes in various geographic locations and can happen to either gender. To prove the myth that only poor, uneducated women are abused is incorrect, I've composed a list of rich, famous people, who have suffered abuse during their lifetime. They are as follows: Halle Berry, Charlize Theron, Rihanna, Drew Barrymore, Madonna, Christina Aguilera, Pamela Anderson, Marilyn Monroe, Oprah, Bill Clinton, Tyler Perry, Rosie O'Donnell, Eleanor Roosevelt, Roseanne Barr, Richard Nixon, Jewel, Chevy Chase, Queen Latifah, Marilyn Manson, Janice Dickinson, Fiona Apple, Dave Mustaine, Maya Angelou, Henry Rollins, Missy Elliott, Axel Rose, Tavis Smiley, Tina Turner, Mariah Carey, Diane Lane, Rosie Perez, George Orwell, Gabriel Byrne, Antwone Fisher, Robert Blake, Jonathan Davis, Mary J. Blige, Joyce Meyer, Erin Gray, Carlos Santana, Kirk Hammett, Lee Daniels, Fantasia, Maynard James Keenan, Rain Pryor, Duane Lee Chapman, Derek Luke, Mike Patton, Shakira, and Pat Conroy (Ranker, 2019 & Ranker, 2021). The ugliness of abuse has no boundaries. Hence, any person could become a victim.

The second myth is that "[v]ictims provoke and deserve the violence they experience." The truth is that the perpetrator is accountable for the unacceptable behavior of domestic violence, and the victim is not to blame in this situation. The third myth is that "[v]ictims of domestic violence move from one abusive relationship to another." Most victims of domestic violence do not seek abusive partners, but unfortunately, there is a higher probability of domestic violence for victims, who were domestically abused as children. The fourth myth is "[v]ictims of domestic violence suffer from low self-esteem and psychological disorders." In reality, "some victims of domestic violence experience a decrease in self-esteem because their abusers are constantly degrading, humiliating, and criticizing them, which . . . makes them more vulnerable to staying in the relationship." The last and final myth is "[v]ictims of domestic violence are weak and always want help." This is a misnomer; victims may be scared to leave the perpetrator for fear of what he or she may do.

# CHAPTER TEN
## PSYCHOLOGICAL PERSPECTIVE

## PERSONALITY DISORDERS THAT COULD NEGATIVELY IMPACT YOUR RELATIONSHIP

To truly understand people, it is useful to appreciate some basic psychology, but more importantly, comprehension of psychological disorders and their symptoms can help us navigate away from relationships, which might become volatile. The American Psychological Association's Diagnostic and Statistical Manual of Mental Disorders (DSM-5) describes psychiatric disorders. I will briefly discuss each disorder, so you will have a basic knowledge of the major indicators of each. This chapter comes with a warning to not overgeneralize or try diagnosing anyone, since diagnosis should come directly from a licensed medical professional. This chapter is simply an overview of the major disorders and their symptoms (American Psychological Association, n.d.).

### Levels of Personality Functioning

Additionally, according to the American Psychological Association, there are five levels from healthy (0) to extreme impairment (4) in the levels of personality functioning. Likewise, there are two domains that are used to determine a person's level of functioning. The self-domain contains the categories, which are identity (the individual has an understanding that they are unique, and they have a clear boundary that they live by) and self-direction (the pursuit of goals in life). The interpersonal domain contains the categories of empathy (tolerance of different perspectives) and intimacy (mutual regard for others). A highly functioning individual would have appropriate boundaries in relationships, would set reasonable goals, would be able to appreciate different perspectives, and would be able to maintain caring relationships. On the other hand, an individual who is low functioning will have a weak self-image, feel they are persecuted, is incapable of understanding others' perspectives, and has a consistently negative engagement with others (American Psychological Association, n.d.).

## Major Personality Disorders

In addition to understanding personality functioning, it is useful to know the symptoms of major personality disorders. Hence, if your partner is low functioning and suffers from one or more personality disorders, your life with them will be difficult. Individuals can also suffer from one or more personality disorders, which will compound any relationship issues. Below is a  discussion of the major personality disorders, so you can become aware of the symptoms.

## Paranoid Personality Disorder

Individuals suffering from this disorder will be generally distrustful and suspicious of others. There are seven indicators of this personality disorder. This individual will be suspicious of others causing them harm without reason. The person will be engrossed in the doubts of people being trustworthy, will not disclose information for fear of it being unkindly used against them, and will consider benign remarks as having a demeaning or threatening meaning. The person will hold grudges, will feel their character is attacked when no one else perceives a threat, and will have repeated suspicions of their partner's fidelity (American Psychological Association, n.d.).

## Schizoid Personality Disorder

Individuals suffering from this disorder will be generally detached from social relationships and will not be able to appropriately express emotions. There are seven indicators of this personality disorder. This individual will not desire or appreciate close relationships. The person will prefer solitary activities, does not want a sexual experience with others, and does not experience pleasure with most activities. The person does not have close friends, is indifferent to praise or criticism, and is emotionally detached (American Psychological Association, n.d.).

## Schizotypal Personality Disorder

Individuals suffering from this disorder will generally be deficient in social and interpersonal relationships due to cognitive and perceptual distortions. This individual will have odd beliefs, will suffer from strange perceptual experiences, and will have odd thoughts and speech. The person will be suspicious, will have an inappropriate affect, and will have odd behavior. The person will have a lack of close friends and will suffer an unwarranted social anxiety (American Psychological Association 2012).

## Antisocial Personality Disorder

Individuals suffering from this disorder will have a "disregard for and violation of the rights of others" (APA, n.d., 1). The individual will fail to conform to social norms, will be deceitful, and will be impulsive. The person will be aggressive and irritable, will have no regard for safety, will be irresponsible, and will have a lack of remorse (American Psychological Association, n.d.).

## Borderline Personality Disorder

Individuals suffering from this disorder will have a "pervasive pattern of instability of interpersonal relationships, self-image, and affect" (APA, n.d., 1). The individual will work to avoid abandonment, will have a "pattern of unstable and intense interpersonal relationships characterized by alternating between extremes of idealization and devaluation" (APA, n.d., 1), and will have an unstable of sense of self. Likewise, the person will be impulsive, will have recurrent self-destructive behavior, emotional instability, and "chronic feelings of emptiness" (APA, n.d., 1). The person will have intense displays of anger and can have severe dissociative symptoms (American Psychological Association, n.d.).

## Histrionic Personality Disorder

Individuals suffering from this disorder will be excessively emotional. The individual will need to be the center of attention, behave provocatively, and will shift emotions rapidly. The individual will use their physical appearance to gain attention, lacks detail in speech, and is theatrical. The person is easily influenced and "considers relationships to be more intimate than they actually are" (American Psychological Association, n.d., 1).

## Narcissistic Personality Disorder

Individuals suffering from this disorder will have a "grandiose sense of self-importance, will have fantasies of limitless success, and feels as if they are elite" (p. 1). The individual needs excessive admiration, a sense of entitlement, and exploits others. Likewise, the person will lack empathy for others, will be envious, and will act arrogant (American Psychological Association, n.d.).

## Avoidant Personality Disorder

Individuals suffering from this disorder will be socially inhibited. The individual will evade occupational events, will be reluctant to spend time with others unless they are convinced, will fear being shamed in intimate relationships, and will be preoccupied with social rejection. Likewise, the person will be inhibited interpersonally, will feel inferior, and will be averse to taking risks (American Psychological Association, n.d.).

# Dependent Personality Disorder

Individuals suffering from this disorder will be indicated by clinging behavior. The individual is indecisive, is unable to assume responsibility, is agreeable to avoid disapproval of others, and lacks self-confidence, so they will not initiate activities. Likewise, this type of person will go to excessive lengths to gain the support of others, feels helpless when alone, needs to always be in a relationship, and fears having to take care of oneself (American Psychological Association, n.d.).

## Obsessive-Compulsive Personality Disorder

Individuals suffering from this disorder will have a "pattern of preoccupation with orderliness, perfectionism, and mental and interpersonal control, at the expense of flexibility, openness, and efficiency" (APA, n.d., 1). The individual is fanatical with rules and order, perfectionism that thwarts progress, excludes personal activities for work productivity, and is over conscientious. Likewise, the person keeps items that are no longer valuable, is reluctant to delegate tasks, is miserly with money, and is rigid (American Psychological Association, n.d.).

## Depressive Personality Disorder

Individuals suffering from this disorder will have depressive thoughts. The individual's mood is depressive, has feelings of inadequacy, is critical of oneself, and is full of worry. Likewise, the person is negativistic, pessimistic, and remorseful (American Psychological Association, n.d.).

## Passive-Aggressive Personality Disorder

Individuals suffering from this disorder will have a "pervasive pattern of negative attitudes and passive resistance to demands for adequate performance" (APA, n.d., 1). The individual passively resists completing tasks, feels misunderstood, is argumentative, and scorns authority. Likewise, the person has resentment for fortunate people, has complaints of misfortune, and "[a]lternates between hostile defiance and contrition" (American Psychological Association, n.d., 1).

This book is meant to give you an idea of what type of person to pursue by giving you an awareness of the different types of people that are available in the world. Some individuals can fall into more than one category. What you need to keep in mind is, if the negatives outweigh the positive aspects of the person, it may be in your best interest to cut your losses and move on to another mate. Humans are very complex beings, so this information is simply meant to serve as a guide and not an end all for determining the right person for you. Additionally, even the best people and relationships will require work, compromise, and understanding to continue. This is not meant to stereotype anyone. It is simply meant to point out some of the challenges faced with a particular type of person. Of course, human beings are very complex and cannot be simply explained away by a simple description. Everyone brings their prior experiences into the relationship, which includes their values, beliefs, and their perspective on the world. The vital aspect of this situation is that you find someone, who respects your way of life, and you respect their way of life.

## Quality Person

It is difficult to find a quality individual. When we are younger, we have less understanding of the world and are much more likely to settle for someone, who is less than desirable. Sometimes, it takes the wisdom of time and years to realize what's important in life. A partner should possess the ability to give you the support and freedom to flourish without competing with you, displaying jealousy, or petty foolishness. A true partner will love and respect you by being supportive of your wants and desires. Hence, a quality person is someone, who is whole within themselves, and they can be supportive of you being whole, too.

# Divorced Person

The divorced person comes to the relationship with a stack of luggage. Every individual is impacted by their past relationships, just as your fears, concerns, and preconceptions are correlated to your past relationships. How damaged the person is will be determined by the trauma experienced in their previous relationship. In the following scenarios, you can switch the gender roles according to your type of relationship (i.e., male to female, female to male, male to male, female to female).

For instance, a divorced man, who was cheated on by his wife, will of course, have a low level of trust for women and will more than likely want to keep them at an emotional distance. He will be very vulnerable because he is unable to trust, thanks to his ex-wife. It may take him a while, or he may never recover from the damage done in his previous relationship. If he is someone whom you see all your preferred qualities in, let him know that you are interested in him, but do not count on the relationship going very far until he has healed from the pain that was inflicted upon him. Know that he may have difficulty committing to more than a date here and there. This man may go out with you on a date and then barely talk to you for weeks at a time. He may seem to have his life together on the outside, but truth be known, he fears opening himself up again to a woman because she may destroy him like his ex-wife did when she cheated on him.

Although this situation can be difficult, if you really like him and you are extremely patient, you just might have a chance to work a relationship with him, but it will take a lot of work on your part and a lot of healing on his part. He will need a lot of reassurance and to know that once in a committed relationship and that you will not stray. On the other hand, he may never be ready for a committed relationship with you, so you need to be very careful as to how much time and energy you invest in any type of relationship with him. The best choice in some cases is simply to be his friend and to get to know him better. If you are meant to be together, it will happen naturally, but if not, you have gained a friend in the process.

Another consideration of dating a divorced man comes into play if he has children. How a man treats his children and talks about them will give you good insight into what kind of man he is. Does he value the same things that you do? Does he have a similar parenting style? Once again, it is prudent to have a relationship with someone who has similar values. Additionally, he will always be tied to the ex-wife, if they have children together, which could be a difficult situation depending upon the dynamics of their relationship. Many people are bitter toward their ex, so this can compound difficulties in a relationship. How he behaves with his ex-wife or ex-paramour is very telling as to what type of man he is. Is he patient and level-headed when dealing with her? Does he always keep in mind that how he treats her will impact his children, or does he talk badly about her in front of them? Always keep the end in mind. If you begin a relationship with a man, who treats his ex-wife or ex-girlfriend with disrespect in front of his children, know that history has a way of repeating itself. Years down the road, you could be his ex-wife, and you could be the object of the discontent in his life. So, choose carefully and be very certain that you will not regret your choice.

An additional issue involved in dating a man with children is a matter of logistics. Trying to coordinate special time together can be like trying to pass legislation; it's a long and hard process that does not always result in a win-win situation for everyone involved. It's important to identify very early on what your schedule situation is going to be because it will be a futile effort if you are unable to coordinate quality time together.

Likewise, children place a new factor into the whole process of dating, so take it slow and don't rush into a relationship. In fact, it would be prudent to not meet the children until you know that this relationship is going somewhere. Children are easily damaged when they become attached to people in their inner circle, and given that their parents are divorced, they may suffer from separation anxiety, so be cautious in this situation. Of course, this same consideration should be given to your children, as well.

## The Lifelong Bachelor / Bachelorette

This person has made a lifestyle of meeting their needs without committing to a legally bound relationship. They may have issues of inadequacy that prevent them from being capable of loving or caring for another human being besides themself. They may have had a traumatic childhood that creates fear around committed relationships. They may have focused on career and put relationships low on their priority list. They may be commitment phobic and, as a result, they may run from committed relationships or may keep strong boundaries up to protect their emotional well-being. Another possible reason why they are a bachelor or bachelorette is that they have not found the perfect mate for them, yet. Or, they may have been unlucky in love. Maybe, they were engaged, but things did not work out. Human relationships are quite complex, so keep an open mind. There is no judgement here because everyone must do what is right for them. Just a word of caution, if you need a lot of tender loving care and you get into a relationship with an individual, who is emotional unavailable, you will be dissatisfied with your relationship. Remember, emotional distance is a red flag in a relationship.

## Type A Person

If you start dating someone, who has a Type A personality, you may feel a bit lonely in your relationship. You may be asking the question why. The answer is that a person with Type A personality will be totally dedicated to their job and may not realize the importance of having a work-life balance. Hence, your relationship may suffer due to being put second to all work-related activities. A Type A personality requires more control than most other personalities. If you are a very self-sufficient, independent and you do not require a great deal of tender loving care (TLC), a Type A partner may be a good mate for you.

## Coworker

Beware of dating coworkers. President Bill Clinton and many others have suffered from the aftereffects of having chosen a sexual partner simply out of proximity. As Americans, we work a great deal of time, so it makes perfect sense that we would start to find the people we work with attractive. The warning is to resist the urge to move forward with a relationship with a coworker, since the repercussions can be devastating to your career and life, depending upon the situation.

First, there could possibly be a change of status for you if you partake in relationships of this sort. For example, if you are having an affair with your boss, which should be considered the ultimate mistake, you could be perceived as sleeping your way to the top. Hence, people, especially your subordinates, will not have much respect for you. Likewise, it will be difficult to determine whether your gains at work are due to sleeping with your boss or your own efforts at doing your job well. The next possible downfall to having a relationship with a coworker is that if the relationship goes nowhere, you are stuck looking at that person daily, which will probably be uncomfortable. There is a strong warning against beginning a relationship with a coworker because it will complicate more than one area of your life.

## Social Climber

Beware the user and social climber. Sometimes, one partner will prey on the other to gain high-status in life. They are looking for a way to improve their status in life by finding a successful person, who can enhance their financial standing. There is no reason for a man or woman to have the need to know your income level or the amount of wealth you have. If he or she asks you about your financial status, beware. This type of person is not the worst type of human being by any means, but the questioning of your financial status should elicit apprehension as to why your income and assets are any of their concern.

Maybe, they have been financially hurt by a partner in the past, so they want assurance that you are self-sufficient and are not a gold digger. On the other hand, maybe you are making more money than them or have more status, so it may emasculate them. We see this happen when an actors and actresses get married. When her career takes off and his doesn't, he may feel a certain way about it and as a result, they get divorced. The point to be made here is that nobody needs to know your financial status unless they are processing your taxes, legal matters, or they are completing a real estate transaction for you. I strongly recommend that you do not mix business with pleasure. Hence, you should not have a relationship with your lawyer, accountant, real estate agent, or loan officer because they hold too much knowledge about your financial standing, and knowledge is power. This information would be to their advantage and could be used to manipulate you.

Regardless of the situation, always protect your financial standing. If you decide to get married, be certain to have your significant other sign a prenuptial agreement. If he or she truly loves you, signing a prenuptial agreement will not bother him. Times have changed, not only do men need to protect themselves financially, but so do women. For example, a San Diego woman (i.e., Crystal Harris) was ordered to pay alimony to her husband who had been jailed for sexually assaulting her while they were married (ABC's Nightline April 5, 2012, 1). The advice here is to protect your financial standing by not falling for a "gold digger" and protecting yourself through a prenuptial agreement.

## Dubious Person

In life, the abused begin to feel they have somehow caused their abuse or that they deserve it. They begin to form negative emotions, which are turned inward, and as a result, they walk through life with caution by avoiding the opportunity to strive for a better way of life. Each of life's disappointments reinforces the concept of unworthiness. This can be seen in men and women, who have low self-esteem and do not apply themselves in life. They often have difficulty sticking with any one path in life and live a rather scattered existence. In addition to the low level of self-esteem, this person will be sensitive to others' feelings and, at times, may be an extremely emotional person. This person's emotions are easily displayed and may make them appear to be weak. Again, there is no judgement here because each person regardless of gender has both masculine and feminine energies. Some people identify with a stronger feminine, others identify with a strong masculine, and some people can balance between their feminine and masculine energy.

The display of emotions will change the power in the relationships. What I mean is, one person in each relationship will be more dominant than the other. If you are a woman in the relationship with an extremely emotional man, then you as the woman would possibly take on the more of a masculine role in the relationship and the man would possibly take on a more feminine role or vice versa. Unless, both partners have balanced their masculine and feminine energies one will be more masculine, and one will be more feminine.

## Abusive Person

Being in a relationship can be the greatest, most fulfilling experience or the most exasperating, annoying experience in your life, depending upon your partner. The warning here is to choose carefully and be certain the person you are with is the right for you. This section is meant to help you identify and pay attention to the warning signs long before you are in a committed relationship.

The trifecta of terror refers to the three major issues that can be experienced in a relationship. The first is a jealous person, who will always be suspicious of you and others. The second is a controlling person, who must have everything their way. Finally, the deconstructive person, who destroys their partner through negative verbal abuse. I refer to these three types of issues as the trifecta of terror because the most under desirable partner will have not only one of these behavior types, but all three. To make matters worse, each one of these issues appear to get progressively worse over time and can move from verbal abuse to emotional abuse and then graduating to physical abuse. Hence, if your partner makes you feel bad about yourself by stating mean, hateful, or hurtful things about you and to you, you may not be in the right relationship. It is better to exit this relationship sooner rather than later and protect yourself from unnecessary hurt.

## Jealous Person

If you're dating a person and they share with you that they get jealous proceed with caution. Depending upon the degree of jealousy, you may decide that you cannot have a relationship with them. Jealousy is born out of insecurity and a lack of trust. Since trust is a paramount characteristic of a positive relationship, beware. Deal breakers in a relationship with a jealous person, would be if the individual's jealousy causes physical outbursts or if their jealousy is directed at your children. No relationship should have to be a balance between your partner and your children because your children should always come first.

## Controlling Person

If you're dating a controlling person and they find something wrong with almost everything you and others do and say, beware! This type of person will break you down psychologically until you are a shell of your former self. You may even start to doubt yourself until you reflect upon the situation and recognize how uncomfortable this relationship is. Regardless of how rich, educated, or street-smart you may be, a person like this is toxic and will do their best to break you down, so they can feel superior to you. It will not matter how nice and caring you are toward them. They will criticize you to the point that you can barely even recognize yourself because they will have negatively affected your self-image. A relationship must have reciprocity on all levels, so be careful.

In essence, a relationship with a controlling person will have you living for nothing more than this person's needs and desires. Thus, your life will be the endless pursuit of their happiness. A controlling partner will require 95 to 100 percent of your attention to meet their demands and requirements. They may require you to "check in" with them on all your daily activities. They may organize their house in a very specific way and will require that you follow their rules to a "tee." They might even require obsessive cleanliness and orderliness to always be maintained. They may run their house as if it is a military base and they are the Commanding Officer. In extreme cases, they may set the house rules and enforce the punishments, which may be severe in nature either verbally or—even worse—physically, if not obeyed.

Likewise, they may make it difficult for you to maintain relationships with your family and friends. You may be asking yourself, why would it be difficult for me to maintain any relationship except the relationship with him? Well, here's how it works. It starts with simple comments about how they dislike this or that about your friends or family. Then over time, you find it easier to simply avoid friends and family as opposed to hearing your partner complain or argue with you about them. Slowly, they isolate you to the point that you are completely alone, and they have full control of your life.

Similarly, they may act as if they are the only person that matters, and they may have no reservation about telling you that you don't know anything; regardless of how educated you are or how ignorant they are. This type of person is totally self-absorbed and incapable of empathy for anyone's plight but their own. If you see the warning signs, address the issues before it's too late. What I mean by too late is that you have married the person, or you have had a child with them. Below are some warning signs of a controlling person:

1. They isolate you.

2. They insult or belittle you.

3. They constantly correct you.

4. They criticizes everything you do.

5. They degrade you with their actions.

6. They dislike your family and friends.

7. They have no respect for your feelings.

8. They're obsessive about cleanliness and orderliness.

There is nothing they won't do to keep control over you, so be careful of this person and their behavior. They will usually only have their interests in mind with all decisions made and this is where the problems begin in the relationship. At the point, you start questioning why everything must be their way, they will immediately get angry at you because they will feel they are losing control. They will do whatever it takes to get you "back in line." In this type of relationship, you will feel like a child, and they will feel more like a parent, who's telling you how you should behave (i.e., it's either their way or it's wrong). This type of person may become physically abusive. If they can convince you that you are the problem, they have won. Controlling partners count on the fact that breaking their victim down emotionally will make them easier to control. Hence, their control, becomes your prison, and they are a relentless warden.

The realization of being in a controlling relationship may not occur quickly. Remember, I discussed the public persona that people display and the fact that they do not reveal their true authentic self until later in the relationship. A controller will work on their victim slowly over time and then will eventually reveal their true self. Sometimes, family and friends pick up on the danger signs of this individual long before the person in the relationship realizes it.

The problem lies in the fact that by this time, he or she has been actively justifying their partner's behavior to family and friends. Psychologically, the victim has vested their partner as being a 'good person'. Thus, he or she may be likely to stay in this bad relationship when they should get out sooner rather than later. It is important that the individual swallows their pride as opposed to staying in this abusive relationship that will continue to break them down daily.

## Deconstructive Partner

The next type of person is the deconstructive partner, who is simply toxic. Most of what they say to others is venomous. They are often judgmental and rigid in their beliefs. They can be extremely difficult to work with in any type of situation, since they tend to see life from their perspective only. They can be oppositional to anything and everything that is not their way of doing things. The deconstructive partner thrives on tearing down their victims. This individual will criticize everything. They will tell you there is something wrong with what you say, do, buy, wear, think, and feel. Hence, they will destroy you with their words. Even when you do nice things for them, they will verbally bash everything you do. Hence, there is no pleasing them.

This individual thrives on your pain and has no regard for your feelings. Their put-downs and snide comments are like daggers that may not seem to hurt but left unaddressed, will slowly over time begin to tear you down inside, and that is what they are counting on. They want you to feel just as bad about yourself, as they feel about themselves. As soon as you notice that they are trying this tactic on you, cut them out of your life like a cancer. They are toxic, and they lack the ability to understand the pain they cause. To make matters even worse, they may not even be aware of their atrocious behavior and how it impacts those around them. You are not going to change them regardless of how kind you are to them. Regardless of whether, they are aware of their horrible behavior or not, it is in your best interest to remove yourself from situations that are not for your highest good.

I once knew a couple in which the woman was very sweet and was always tried to please her man. She bought clothes that he said he liked, but he always found fault with how they fit, the material, or brand. She would buy food and cook for him, and he would complain about it. He would constantly correct her grammar, what she said, and corrected her comments, which she found to be quite annoying. Then one day, she could no longer take his constant badgering and she kicked him out of her life. It took her a long time to recover from her relationship with him, but she pulled herself together and focused on repairing the damage he had caused on her psyche. Then, one day out of the clear blue, he called to tell her that he loved her. She was shocked and appalled by his confession of love because the only emotions she had seen him display were hatefulness, harsh judgment, and disgust for anything she said and did. After the initial shock wore off, she told him that he had no idea what love was, and she ended their conversation.

A controlling person feels inadequate, so they thrive on getting their demands met while verbally, emotionally, and/or physically abusing their partners. Usually, the abuse starts slowly and progresses over time. If you let them abuse you once and you do not take measures to address the abuse, they will continue to abuse you. Why? According to behavioral psychology, the behavior (i.e., their abuse) will continue to occur if they are not confronted and punished for it immediately. Hence, their behavior is reinforced when you stay with them, and they get away with abusing you. Thus, they will more than likely abuse you again in the future, and there is a high probability that the abuse will get progressively worse over time.

They will continue to hurt you if you let him. The abuser is not likely to have self-awareness of how their comments and actions impact you, nor will they care. Abusers usually suffer from some sort of inadequacy, which makes them lash out at others to make themselves feel better. By inadequacy, I mean they could suffer from low self-esteem, jealousy, and feelings of being less than others, which fuels their rage. When they are irritated, they are likely to take it out on those closest to them and those who are the weakest. Not all of their abuse comes in the form of physical contact, but whether it is emotional or physical, the result is the same; it hurts the victims. In some cases, the abuser flies into rages and takes it out on loved ones, only to feel remorseful a few minutes later; either way it is unacceptable.

The warning here is that abusers continue to abuse. It is not a matter of how much you love them or the fact that you think you are special enough to make them change. Never think that you are going to change another person. A person only changes if they want to change. So, my advice to you is to understand and accept people for who they are. If he or she is not what you are looking for move along and save your time and energy for the relationship that you want.

## Negative Person

If your person tries to keep you from advancing and progressing in life, then they do not have your best interest at heart. Usually, people, who are not supportive of their partners, suffer from inferiority complex, which makes them feel bad about themselves. Hence, these individuals strive to keep others around them down, so they can feel better about themselves. This type of abuse can take many forms. This person will find a way to guide you away from your dreams, aspirations, or desires by making you believe negative things about yourself that are simply not true. For example, many years ago, I had a negative man tell me that I would never make it if I went to college. I clearly proved this negative man wrong since not only did I go to college, but I obtained a doctoral degree. Maybe he was intimidated by the idea that I might be smarter than him or that I would leave him behind if I succeeded. Either way, I knew a relationship with him was clearly not in my best interest. I did in fact leave the relationship upon the realization that not only did he not want me to strive for a better life, but he also had no desire to strive for a better life for himself.

# CHAPTER ELEVEN
# COMPATIBILITY

Sometimes you simply must accept the realization that regardless of how much you are attracted to someone, and they may be attracted to you, it may not be meant to be. I had a friend who was entirely smitten with this man. They had great conversations and got along well, but there was always a missing component to their relationship. There was chemistry between them, but it was not enough to constitute a basis for a relationship. He appeared to have all the qualities that she looked for in a man, but there was a missing element that she could not determine, and for that, she knew that they would never be any more than friends. Although he was a nice guy, she was leery of him as he had been hurt in a relationship, and she was not sure how deep the damage was and if it was what caused him to seem fickle. Upon coming to the realization that nothing was going to come of this relationship, she distanced herself from him, and life went on for both.

According to Dr. John Gottman, there are certain destructive behaviors that are responsible for causing couples to separate. He refers to these negative behaviors as "The Four Horsemen of the Apocalypse" (p. 1). The first negative behavior is criticism, which is complaining about your partner. Contempt is the second and most damaging behavior in a relationship, and it occurs when one partner makes statements as if they are superior to their partner. The third negative behavior is defensiveness

and is a form of self-protection. The final destructive behavior is stonewalling, which is the emotional withdrawal from situations.

If you are dating and you as a couple have difficulty agreeing on little things, you should think twice about continuing your relationship. The right relationship does not take a lot of work because you will have trust, good communication, and respect for each other. If you are in a relationship and every argument is solved by you making concessions and the other person always getting their way, you are not in the right relationship.

# ASTROLOGICAL COMPATIBILITY

Human beings are very complex, and thus, there are many factors that will play into whether a relationship will be positive or negative. Some people believe that astrological compatibility plays into every type of relationship. I'm not promoting nor denying the possibilities of compatibility based on astrological signs, but I will go over the main points of each sign. Keep in mind that each person has a Sun, Moon, Venus, and Rising sign will impact the person's behavior. So, astrological compatibility is not as distinct as some may believe.

## Capricorn

Capricorn is the first sign of the calendar year for people born from December 23 through January 19. Capricorns are known for being predictable and independent. They are also known to suppress their emotions. Positive traits of Capricorns are that they are fair and logical. Negative traits or characteristics of Capricorns are that they are stubborn and possibly depressive. In a relationship, they are known to be loyal and reliable partners (Astrology Mini Chart, n.d.). Capricorns are most compatible with partners who are either Taurus or Virgos. They are somewhat compatible with partners who are under the sign of Aquarius, Pisces, Scorpio, or Sagittarius. Capricorns are slightly compatible with the signs of Gemini, Leo, or Capricorn. They should avoid relationships with people who have the signs of Aries, Cancer, or Libra (Thiessen, n.d.).

## Aquarius

Aquarius are born from January 20 through February 19. Aquarians are known for being unconventional and open-minded. Positive traits of an Aquarius are that they are tolerant and idealistic. Their negative traits are that they are cold and unforgiving. When in a relationship, they are faithful if they have freedom (Astrology Mini Chart, n.d.). Aquarius are most compatible with partners who are Gemini, Libra, or Aquarius.

They are somewhat compatible with partners who are under the sign of Pisces, Aries, Sagittarius, or Capricorn. Aquarius are slightly compatible with the signs of Cancer or Virgo. They should avoid relationships with people who have the signs of Taurus, Leo, or Scorpio (Thiessen, n.d.).

## Pisces

Pisces are born from February 20 to March 20. They are easygoing, affectionate, and submissive in nature. Positive traits of the Pisces are that they are gentle and patient. Negative traits are that they are unreliable and careless. When in a relationship, they are romantic and loyal (Astrology Mini Chart, n.d.). Pisces are most compatible with partners who are Cancer, Scorpio, or Pisces. They are somewhat compatible with partners who are under the sign of Aries, Taurus, Capricorn, or Aquarius. Pisces are slightly compatible with the signs of Leo or Libra. They should avoid relationships with people who have the signs of Gemini, Virgo, or Sagittarius (Thiessen, n.d.).

## Aries

Aries are born from March 21 to April 20. Aries are known to be enthusiastic and energetic. Positive traits of Aries are outgoing. Negative traits of Aries are that they are bad tempered and rigid. When in a relationship, they are dominated by an emotional life (Astrology Mini Chart, n.d.). Aries are most compatible with partners who are either Leo or Sagittarius. They are somewhat compatible with partners who are under the sign of Taurus, Gemini, Aquarius, or Pisces. Aries are slightly compatible with the signs of Virgo or Scorpio. They should avoid relationships with people who have the signs of Cancer, Libra, Capricorn, or Aries (Thiessen, n.d.).

## Taurus

Taurus are born between April 21 and May 21. They are known to be gentle and even tempered. Their positive traits are that they are practical and loyal. Their negative traits are that they can be melancholic and, if provoked, very violent. When in a relationship, they are straightforward and can become very jealous (Astrology Mini Chart, n.d.). Taurus are most compatible with partners who are either Virgo or Capricorn. They are somewhat compatible with partners who are under the sign of Gemini, Cancer, Pisces, Aries, or Taurus. Taurus are slightly compatible with the signs of Libra or Sagittarius. They should avoid relationships with people who have the signs of Aquarius, Leo, or Scorpio (Thiessen, n.d.).

## Gemini

Gemini are born between May 22 and June 22. They are known to shift their outlook and be very intelligent. Their positive attributes are that they are happy and affectionate. Their negative traits are that they can be unconscientious and dishonest. When in a relationship, they are liable to fall in and out of love quickly (Astrology Mini Chart, n.d.). Gemini are most compatible with partners who are Libra, Aquarius, or Gemini. They are somewhat compatible with partners who are under the sign of Cancer, Leo, Aries, or Taurus. Gemini are slightly compatible with the signs of Scorpio or Capricorn. They should avoid relationships with people who have the signs of Virgo, Sagittarius, or Pisces (Thiessen, n.d.).

## Cancer

Cancers are born between June 23 and July 23. They are generally known to be sensitive and conservative. Their positive traits are that they are energetic and inspired. Their negative attributes are that they are hurt very easily and are known to withdraw. They are known to have long-term relationships (Astrology Mini Chart, n.d.). Cancers are most compatible with partners who are either Scorpio or Pisces. They are somewhat compatible with partners who are under the sign of Leo, Virgo, Taurus, or Gemini. Cancers are slightly compatible with the signs of Sagittarius or Aquarius. They should avoid relationships with people who have the signs of Libra, Capricorn, Aries, or Cancer (Thiessen, n.d.).

## Leo

Leos are born between July 24 and August 23. They are known to have personal magnetism, to be extroverts, and to be outgoing. Their positive attributes are that they are courageous and self-confident. Their negative traits are that they are arrogant and suspicious. Leos are known to make loyal partners (Astrology Mini Chart, n.d.). Leos are most compatible with partners who are either Sagittarius or Aries. They are somewhat compatible with partners who are under the sign of Virgo, Libra, Gemini, or Cancer. Leos are slightly compatible with the signs of Capricorn, Pisces, or Leo. They should avoid relationships with people who have the signs of Scorpio, Aquarius, or Taurus (Thiessen, n.d.).

## Virgo

Virgos are born from August 24 until September 23. They are generally known to be practical and to act. Their negative attributes are that they are critically inclined and unsophisticated. When in a relationship, they are known to keep tight control over their emotions (Astrology Mini Chart, n.d.). Virgos are most compatible with partners who are Capricorn, Taurus, or Virgo. They are somewhat compatible with partners who are under the sign of Libra, Scorpio, Cancer, or Leo. Virgos are slightly compatible with the signs of Aquarius or Aries. They should avoid relationships with people who have the signs of Sagittarius, Pisces, or Gemini (Thiessen, n.d.).

## Libra

Libras are born from September 24 to October 23. They are generally known to be even tempered and to seek balance. Their positive attributes are that they are affectionate and sociable. Their negative traits are that they are impatient and indecisive. In relationships, they are balanced. Libras are most compatible with partners who are Aquarius, Gemini, or Libra. They are somewhat compatible with partners who are under the sign of Scorpio, Sagittarius, Leo, or Virgo. Libras are slightly compatible

with the signs of Pisces or Taurus. They should avoid relationships with
people who have the signs of Capricorn, Aries, or Cancer (Thiessen,
n.d.).

## Scorpio

Scorpios are born from October 24 through November 22. They are
known to be reserved and easily hurt. Their positive attributes are that
they are passionate and sensitive. Their negative emotions are that they
are quick to anger and impatient. In a relationship, they can be obsessive
and jealous (Astrology Mini Chart, n.d.). Scorpios are most compatible
with partners who are either Pisces or Cancer. They are somewhat
compatible with partners who are under the sign of Sagittarius,
Capricorn, Virgo, or Libra. Scorpios are slightly compatible with the
signs of Aries or Gemini. They should avoid relationships with people
who have the signs of Aquarius, Taurus, Leo, or Scorpio (Thiessen, n.d.).

## Sagittarius

Sagittarius are born from November 23 until December 22. They are
known to have an open and generous attitude. Their positive attributes
are that they are generous and modest. Their negative attributes are that
they are quick to anger, and they are rigid. When in a relationship, they
are sincere and straightforward, but they lack jealousy and possessiveness
(Astrology Mini Chart, n.d.). Sagittarius are most compatible with
partners who are either Aries or Leo. They are somewhat compatible
with partners who are under the sign of Capricorn, Aquarius, Libra,
or Scorpio. Sagittarius are slightly compatible with the signs of Taurus,
Cancer, or Sagittarius. They should avoid relationships with people who
have the signs of Pisces, Gemini, or Virgo (Thiessen, n.d.).

# HEALTHY RELATIONSHIPS

According to the Iowa Coalition Against Domestic Violence (n.d.), "Healthy relationships are characterized by respect, sharing and trust . . . [; t]hey are based on the belief that both partners are equal, that the power and control in the relationship are equally shared" (p. 1). A relationship should have R-E-S-P-E-C-T. A respectful relationship should be a display of affection and caring between partners. Equality should be present in all matters of life (i.e., a sharing of responsibilities). They must be supportive of each other's goals and aspirations (i.e., both partners work toward their potential in life); passionate in that the partners truly care deeply for each other; empathetic by understanding each other's feelings and opinions; and have communication that is open and considerate. Trust should be present in that both partners are valued and treated with the utmost admiration.

## Respect

One of the most important characteristics of a relationship is respect. If you do not have respect from the person, you're in a relationship with, you should not be in this relationship. Respect is the foundation of any relationship that allows for you to feel safe and loved. As the old saying goes, "You must give respect to get respect." Unfortunately, many people demand respect, but they are unable to give respect.

## Equality

There is a sharing of responsibilities of household duties and childcare. Each partner should have access to transportation. Both partners have the freedom to aspire to their goals in life by attending school or working. They work together to accomplish common goals. There should be reciprocity in that there is an equal give and take between the partners.

## Supportive

Each partner is supportive of the other's goals. Both partners are willing to make sacrifices, so the other can meet their educational or career goals. Each partner should encourage the other.

## Passionate

Each partner lets the other see just how much they care for them. There should be a strong emotional attachment to the partner and for the partner. There should be a display of love for each other.

## Empathetic

Each partner should understand the other's perspective in life. The partner should understand the other person's way of life. Each partner should feel bad for their partner's pain, suffering, fears, etc.

## Communication

Each partner should be able to express themselves without fear. Both should be able to speak to their partner in a respectful manner. Hence, communication should be a two-way street.

## Trust

Every relationship is based on trust. If trust is not present in your relationship, you do not have a relationship. The trust factor is necessary for any healthy relationship. Trust means that the person you are with is secure with themselves, and they can build you up by supporting your wants and desires rather than breaking you down.

Did your previous relationships have all the elements of the R-E-S-P-E-C-T model? What was missing? What could you do to change your next relationship for the positive?

_______________________________________________

_______________________________________________

_______________________________________________

_______________________________________________

# SUCCESS STORIES

This book has detailed various types of people, the key factors that indicate abuse, and ways of identifying compatibility. As stated previously, human relationships are very complex, so it is good to take a comprehensive perspective when trying to find and keep a relationship. We discussed many pitfalls to avoid when dating; now we're going to discuss what makes a healthy relationship.

There is nothing nicer than a couple who truly cares about each other. It is a rare situation, but I have been fortunate enough to see this bliss a few times in my life. These couples all have the same qualities in their relationships. First, they held their partner in high esteem. Hence, before they made any major changes or choices, they always considered how it would affect their partner and consulted them before any major life choices were made. Not only would they consider their partner's feelings, but they also would gauge life from the perspective of "we" and not "me." I think many problems in relationships stem from not having the ability to see life from the other person's perspective. Think about it: if you constantly make choices, which affect both you and your partner, but you fail to consider how it will impact them, your partner will eventually begin to resent you. In essence, what you are telling them without saying it directly is "I really don't care what you think or how my choices affect you." This can be a difficult thing for your partner to accept especially if you continually make choices without their input and it negatively impacts their well-being.

Next, these couples all displayed a great deal of respect for each other. This is shown in many ways such as not letting discussions disintegrate into arguments. These couples respected their partner's choices in life and were supportive of their dreams and aspirations—even if the attainment of their dreams meant personal sacrifice for both parties. I've seen situations where one partner would forego their own advancement, so the other person could attempt to achieve their goals. Of course, this type of situation was not a one-way street. These couples always found a way to reciprocate the same level of support for their other partner, once the goal set was achieved.

Additionally, these couples maintained understanding for their partner. The understanding came in the form of identifying the apparent differences and not seeing them as a barrier to the relationship but rather a way of allowing each person to be an individual while still maintaining the "we" of a relationship. This can be seen in couples where one really likes sports, and the other does not care that much for sports. There are situations in which the non-sports fan will promote the sports fan to enjoy their preferred sport. This may be accomplished by one partner trying to enjoy the activity with their partner or by creating situations where the partner can enjoy the chosen sport with other people of like mind. For example, a partner could sit down to watch the Sunday football game or get tickets for the partner and their best friend to attend the preferred sporting event. This type of selfless deed not only shows an understanding for the partner but will shows how much they care about the person and their happiness.

Likewise, these couples maintained a team relationship. Sometimes, they had an unspoken air about them that exuded an almost us-against-the-world type of togetherness. It seemed that they had created a synergy of "we can get through anything as long as we are together." It is strange, but it seems that they have a connection that goes much deeper than most couples can achieve.

Finally, and most importantly, couples who are successful in their relationships maintain a great deal of trust for each other. It does not matter how much time they are apart; they are committed to their partner. To have and maintain mutual trust is paramount to the relationship. Since trust is the cornerstone of any relationship, a healthy level of trust in their partner is maintained using direct communication of needs. Couples who are open and direct in their communication about what they need and want are more likely to stay together because they will not need to go outside the relationship to fulfill their wants, needs, and desires.

Several characteristics equate to a lasting relationship. First, holding your partner in high esteem and always considering their feelings in your choices will reinforce positive feelings in the relationship. Next, having a great deal of respect for your partner and their beliefs and choices will lead to mutual respect since usually, if you give respect, you get respect. Likewise, maintaining understanding for your partner will open the lines of communication and help build the connection between you and him. Similarly, partners who have close connections will form a team-like perspective, so each partner knows they will not face any situation without the full support of their partner. Finally, a strong sense of trust between partners will lend well to the relationship enduring over time.

Your relationship partner should be supportive. A relationship is not a competition, it is a partnership in which each partner supports the other. Partners should not seek to control one another because love does not control. It does not matter what you have done in the past; everyone deserves love. There is no excuse for you to accept being mistreated or being dissatisfied in your life. Each person has something positive to contribute to the world. Likewise, each person has the right to be treated with respect, dignity, and tender loving care. The trip through life is much more enjoyable when you have a person to walk through it with, who loves you and treats you well. Hence, you deserve love, and I hope this book will help you find it.

To be loved, you must first love yourself. You must believe that you are worthy of a happy and healthy relationship. If you think you're unworthy of a relationship, you will more than likely choose the wrong partner. You may choose someone you know is well below your standards because you do not feel worthy of someone better, who might treat you good. You must start today, believing that you are worthy of a happy relationship with a person, who will love and take care of you.

In life, we set our own limitations. If you set your expectations low, then you don't leave much room for growth. You must always think that you deserve better in life. Whether this is in your career, your education, or your relationship; you deserve better. In life, we sometimes pick up negative beliefs, and we carry these negative beliefs with us into every relationship we have. You must release yourself from all negative beliefs you have incorporated into your life. Sometimes as children, we experience situations that make us feel less than worthy of happiness. These feelings and beliefs must be released; otherwise, they continue to hold you back in life.

Your experiences have made you, who you are today. If there is any part of you that you do not like or you feel shame, guilt, fear, or anger, start the healing process today. To begin your healing and change your prospective on life and love, you could read *Co-Create Your New Life by Kimberly Lobera.*

# REFERENCES

—.1981. "Traumatic Bonding: The Development of Emotional Attachments in Battered Women and Other Relationships of Intermittent Abuse." Victimology 6: 139-155.

—.1987. "Evaluating Programs for Men Who Batter: Problems and Prospects." Journal of Family Violence 2: 95-108.

—.1989. "The Development of a Measure of Psychological Maltreatment of Women by Their Male Partners." Violence and Victims 4: 159-177.

—.1992b. "The Severity of Violence Against Men Scales." Journal of Family Violence 7: 189-203.

—.2000. "Prevalence and Consequences of Male-to-Female and Female-to-Male Intimate Partner Violence as Measured by the National Violence Against Women Survey." Violence Against Women 6: 142-161.

—2019. 51 Famous Survivors of Child Abuse
Retrieved January 9, 2022, from
https://www.ranker.com/list/famous-survivors-of-child-abuse/celebrity-lists

—2019. 51 Celebrities Who Were Abused
Retrieved January 9, 2022, from
https://www.ranker.com/list/celebrities-who-were-abused/celebrity-lists

ABC's Nightline by Julu Chang and Alyssa Litoff. April 5, 2012. "Sexual Assault Victim Ordered to Pay Alimony to Attacker Fights to Change California Law." Retrieved December 9, 2012, from http://abcnews.

go.com/US/sexual-assault-victim-ordered-pay-alimony-attacker-fights/ story?id=16075409.

Abraham, M. 1999. "Sexual Abuse in South Asian Immigrant Marriages." Violence Against Women 5: 591-618.

American Psychological Association DSM-5 Development. Retrieved November 6, 2012, from http://www.gottman.com/49853/ Research-FAQs.html.

Astrology Mini Chart. n.d. Melbourne, Australia: Dynamo House by Dynamo House Pty. Ltd. Mini Chart, ISBN 9318011000904.

Bergen, R. K. 1996. Wife Rape: Understanding the Response of Survivors and Service Providers. Thousand Oaks, CA: Sage Publications.

Boulette, T. R., and S. M. Andersen. 1986. "'Mind Control' and the Battering of Women." The Cultic Studies Journal 3: 25-34.

Bragg, H. Lien. 2003. Child Protection in Families Experiencing Domestic Violence. Office on Child Abuse and Neglect, Children's Bureau, Caliber Associates.

Brewin, C. R., Cloitre, M., Hyland, P., Shevlin, M., Maercker, A., Bryant, R. A., Reed,G. M. (2017). A review of current evidence regarding the ICD-11 proposals for diagnosing PTSD and complex PTSD. Clinical Psychology Review, 58, 1-15. doi: 10.1016/j.cpr.2017.09.001.

Browne, A. 1987. When Battered Women Kill. New York: Free Press.

Child Welfare Information Gateway. Retrieved November 11, 2012, from http://www.childwelfare.gov/pubs/usermanuals/domesticviolence/ domesticviolencec.cfm.

Cloitre, M., Shevlin M., Brewin, C.R., Bisson, J.I., Roberts, N.P., Maercker, A., Karatzias, T., Hyland, P. (in press). The International Trauma Questionnaire: Development of a self-report measure of ICD-11 PTSD and Complex PTSD. Acta Psychiatrica Scandinavica. DOI: 10.1111/acps.12956

Dutton, D. G., and S. Painter. 1993. "The Battered Woman Syndrome: Effects of Severity and Intermittency of Abuse." American Journal of Orthopsychiatry 63: 614-622.

Finkelhor, D., and K. Yllo. 1985. License to Rape: Sexual Abuse of Wives. New York: Holt, Rinehart, and Winston.

Follingstad, D. R., L. L. Rutledge, B. J. Berg, E. S. Hause, and D. S. Polek. 1990. "The Role of Emotional Abuse in Physically Abusive Relationships." Journal of Family Violence 5: 107-120.

Fremouw, W. J., D. Westrup, and J. Pennypacker. 1997. "Stalking on Campus: The Prevalence and Strategies for Coping with Stalking." Journal of Forensic Science 42: 666-669.

Gondolf, E. W. 1988. "Who Are Those Guys? Toward a Behavioral Typology of Batterers." Violence and Victims 3: 87-203.

Gray, H. M., and V. Foshee. 1997. "Adolescent Dating Violence: Differences between One-Sided and Mutually Violent Profiles." Journal of Interpersonal Violence 12: 126-141.

Harmon, R. B., R. Rosner, and H. Owens. 1998. "Sex and Violence in a Forensic Population of Obsessional Harassers." Psychology, Public Policy, and Law 4: 236-249.

Healing Abused Women. Retrieved November 11, 2012. "Statistics on Abusive Relationships." http://healingabusedwomen.com/2011/07/21/statistics-on-abusive-relationships/.

Hudson, W. W., and S. R. McIntosh. 1981. "The Assessment of Spouse Abuse: Two Quantifiable Dimensions." Journal of Marriage and the Family 43: 873-886.

Hyland, P., Shevlin M., Brewin C.R., Cloitre M., Downes A.J., Jumbe, S., Roberts, N.P. (2017). Validation of post- traumatic stress disorder (PTSD) and complex PTSD using the International Trauma Questionnaire. Acta Psychiatrica Scandinavica. 136, 313-322. doi: 10.1111/acps.12771.

Iowa Coalition Against Domestic Violence. Retrieved November 11, 2012. "Characteristics of Healthy Relationships." http://www. bpdfamily.com/bpdresources/nk_a115.htm.

Karatzias T., Shevlin M., Fyvie C., Hyland P., Efthymiadou E., Wilson D. Cloitre M. (2017). Evidence of distinct profiles of posttraumatic stress disorder (PTSD) and complex posttraumatic stress disorder (CPTSD) based on the new ICD-11 trauma questionnaire (ICD-TQ). Journal of Affective Disorders, 207, 181-187. http://dx.doi.org/10.1016/j. jad.2016.09.032

Koss, M. P., and C. A. Gidycz. 1985. "Sexual Experiences Survey: Reliability and Validity." Journal of Consulting and Clinical Psychology 53: 422-423.

Koss, M. P., L. A. Goodman, A. Browne, L. F. Fitzgerald, G. P. Keita, and N. F. Russo. 1994. No Safe Haven: Male Violence Against Women at Home, at Work, and in the Community. Washington, DC: American Psychological Association.

Koss, M. P., and C. J. Oros. 1982. "Sexual Experiences Survey: A Research Instrument Investigating Sexual Aggression and Victimization." Journal of Consulting and Clinical Psychology 50: 455-457.

Loring, M. T. 1994. Emotional Abuse. New York: Lexington Books.

Mahoney, P., and L. M. Williams. 1998. "Sexual Assault in Marriage: Prevalence, Consequences, and Treatment of Wife Rape. In Partner Violence: A Comprehensive Review of 20 Years of Research, edited by J. L. Jasinski, and L. M. Williams, 113-157. Thousand Oaks, CA: Sage Publications.

Makepeace, J. M. 1986. "Gender Differences in Courtship Violence Victimization." Family Relations 35: 383-388.

Marshall, L. L. 1992a. "Development of the Severity of Violence Against Women Scales." Journal of Family Violence 7: 103-121.

Molina, L. S., and C. Basinait-Smith. 1998. "Revisiting the Intersection between Domestic Abuse and HIV Risk." American Journal of Public Health 88: 1267-1268.

Meloy, J. R., and S. Gothard. 1995. "A Demographic and Clinical Comparison of Obsessional Followers and Offenders with Mental Disorders." American Journal of Psychiatry 152: 258-263.

NiCarthy, G. 1986, 1982. Getting Free: A Handbook for Women in Abusive Relationships. Seattle, WA: Seal Press.

Pan, H. S., P. H. Neidig, and K. D. O'Leary. 1994. "Male-Female and Aggressor-Victim Differences in the Factor Structure of the Modified Conflict Tactics Scale." Journal of Interpersonal Violence 9: 366-382.

Respect.org. Retrieved November 11, 2012, from http://www.loveisrespect.org/is-this-abuse/types-of-abuse?gclid=CLb9_qeuyLMCFWrZQgodeiUAqw.

—.Retrieved November 11, 2012, from http://www.loveisrespect.org/is-this-abuse/why-do-people-stay-in-abusive-relationships.

Russel, D. E. H. 1990. Rape in Marriage. Indianapolis: Indiana University Press.

Romero, M. 1985. "A Comparison between Strategies Used on Prisoners of War and Battered Wives." Sex Roles 13: 537-547.

Shawn. May 1, 2021. (2022 Divorce Rate in America) How Many Marriages End in Divorce Statistics, The Hive Law. Retrieved January 10, 2022, from https://www.thehivelaw.com/blog/divorce-statistics-us-divorce-rate-in-america/

Shepard, M. F., and J. A. Campbell. 1992. "The Abusive Behavior Inventory: A Measure of Psychological and Physical Abuse." Journal of Interpersonal Violence 7: 291-305.

Shevlin, M., Hyland, P., Roberts, N. P., Bisson, J. I., Brewin C.R. & Cloitre M. (2018). A psychometric assessment of Disturbances in Self-Organization symptom indicators for ICD-11 Complex PTSD using the International Trauma Questionnaire, European Journal of Psychotraumatology, 9:1, DOI: 10.1080/20008198.2017.1419749

Stets, J. E. 1991. "Psychological Aggression in Dating Relationships: The Role of Interpersonal Control." Journal of Family Violence 6: 97-114.

Straus, M. A. 1979. "Measuring Intrafamily Conflict and Violence: The Conflict Tactics (CT) Scales." Journal of Marriage and the Family 41: 75-88.

Straus, M. A., and R. J. Gelles. 1986. "Societal Change and Change in Family Violence from 1975 to 1985 as Revealed by Two National Surveys." Journal of Marriage and the Family 48: 465-478.

Straus, M. A., S. L. Hamby, S. Boney-McCoy, and D. B. Sugarman. 1996. "The Revised Conflict Tactics Scales (CTS2): Development and Preliminary Psychometric Data." Journal of Family Issues 17: 283-316.

Thiessen, Michael. n.d. Retrieved November 11, 2012, from http://www. astrology-online.com/quick.htm.

Tjaden, P., and N. Thoennes. 1998. Stalking in America: Findings from the National Violence Against Women Survey. Washington, DC: National Institute of Justice and Centers for Disease Control and Prevention.

Tolman, R. M. 1992. "Psychological Abuse of Women." In Assessment of Family Violence: A Clinical and Legal Sourcebook, edited by R. T. Ammerman, and M. Hersen, 291-310. New York: John Wiley & Sons Inc.

Walker, L. E. 1984. The Battered Woman Syndrome. New York: Springer Publishing Company.

Walker, L. E., and J. R. Meloy. 1998. "Stalking and Domestic Violence." In The Psychology of Stalking: Clinical and Forensic Perspectives, edited by J. R. Meloy, 140-161. San Diego, CA: Academic Press.

Wingood, G. M., and R. J. DiClimente. 1997. "The Effects of an Abusive Primary Partner on the Condom Use and Sexual Negotiation Practices of African-American Women." American Journal of Public Health 87: 1016-1018. May 31, 2005, vol. 11, Issue 7.

www.ingramcontent.com/pod-product-compliance
Lightning Source LLC
Chambersburg PA
CBHW071204300726
48975CB00004B/1278